Love from
Nana & Papa
2018

This book is dedicated to Nanny
from all her charges.

Love Finse

THIS BOOK
BELONGS TO

_____

_____

"Finse of Dogton Abbey - Good Manners"
Based on an idea by Karine Hagen

The right of The Countess of Carnarvon to be identified as the
author and Suzy-Jane Tanner to be identified as the illustrator
of this work has been asserted by them in accordance
with the Copyright Designs and Patents Act 1988.

Text © The Countess of Carnarvon 2015
Illustrations © Suzy-Jane Tanner 2015

First published by Viking Cruises 2015. Reprinted 2016
83 Wimbledon Park Side, London, SW19 5LP

ISBN 978-1-909968-09-7

www.finse.me

Produced by Colophon Digital Projects Ltd,
Old Isleworth, TW7 6RJ, United Kingdom
Printed in China.

Finse of Dogton Abbey
GOOD
MANNERS

The Countess of Carnarvon
Suzy-Jane Tanner

GOOD MANNERS

Grandpup Percy was very happy. His sister, The Dowager Countess of Mantleshelf, was coming to stay at Highclere Castle, my puppyhood home.

We puppies were a little scared. Mummy Bella had told us that she could be very strict. We would have to mind our Ps and Qs!

DIFFERENT DOGS

Grandpup explained to us that this meant behaving politely and being kind and considerate to other dogs.

He also told us that the right and wrong way to do things can be different in other parts of the world, as I had discovered during my travels.

When you are introduced, greet new acquaintances with a firm pawshake.

In more formal situations, you may bow or curtsy.

In parts of Asia, dogs bow their heads with their paws together.

Eskimo dogs rub noses!

Family and friends embrace. When Great Aunt Mantleshelf arrived, she wanted to kiss everyone.

Monroe, Barney, Scoobie and I kissed her back nicely but naughty Alfie did not want to be kissed and rudely turned his face away!

SITTING DOWN TO LUNCH

Before lunch, we washed our paws and faces.

When we sat down at the table, we remembered to sit up straight and place our napkins on our laps.

Except for Monroe, who tied her napkin around her head like a turban. Grandpup growled crossly.

NAUGHTY BOYS

As the special guest, Great Aunt Mantleshelf was served first.

Barney got bored waiting and started to throw bread rolls at Alfie, which was very naughty!

It is polite to wait until everyone has been served before starting to eat but Alfie was rather hungry and had started as soon as he was served his food!

SCOOBIE TAKES TOO MUCH

Scoobie helped himself to a huge plateful. Then he decided he did not like the lunch.

Mummy Bella said it was rude to help yourself to more than you can eat.

Great Aunt Mantleshelf dipped her head to look at Scoobie over her little glasses and Grandpup growled louder.

WHICH KNIFE AND FORK

There were so many knives and forks on the table we didn't know which ones to use. Grandpup explained that we should use the outside ones first then work inwards for each course.

In parts of Asia, dogs eat with chopsticks. There are countries where they eat with their right paw only.

LEAVING THE TABLE

When I had finished eating,
I gathered my knife and fork
together neatly in the middle
of my plate.

You must always ask to be
excused before you leave
the table, though my
brothers hardly ever
remember to do so.

ALFIE GETS STUCK

Alfie had hidden behind the bannisters on the staircase to make his sisters jump with surprise. But he got stuck.

Monroe patiently waited until Grandpup and Great Aunt Mantleshelf had finished talking before she told him what had happened and asked if they could help pull Alfie out.

ALFIE IS NAUGHTY AGAIN

While Grandpup took his afternoon nap, the rest of us went for a walk.

Alfie knew that Monroe hated getting muddy so when she was next to a big puddle he jumped in and splashed her to make her cry.

Mummy Bella got very cross with him again. Alfie was not having a good day.

RESPECT OTHERS

We met Nanny in the Monks' Garden. She could only walk very slowly now, but we loved her.

We rushed to ask her how she was. We didn't mind that we couldn't run so fast when we were with her as she always had such wonderful stories to tell us.

NANNY'S BISCUITS

Great Aunt Mantleshelf had known Nanny for many years and bought her a present of some delicious biscuits.

Nanny asked Mummy Bella if we might have some. We each waited our turn, wagging out tails. She was very fair and we each had just one.

Later in the afternoon, Great Aunt Mantleshelf gave each of us a gift of a proper ink pen.

We were taught to always say 'Please' and 'Thank You' so Monroe used hers straightaway to write a very neat thank you letter holding her pen carefully in her paw. Alfie got ink all over his paws and face, what a surprise!

BE HELPFUL

We were sad when it was time
for Great Aunt Mantleshelf
to go home. Monroe held the
door open and Scoobie and
Barney helped carry her bags.

Even Alfie kissed her nicely
having learnt quite a bit more
about being a good dog. But
he couldn't resist making a
rude face behind her back
afterwards!

GRANDPUP PERCY'S 10 GOLDEN RULES FOR WELL MANNERED PUPPIES.

1 Be kind, considerate and helpful to others.

2 Greet new acquaintances politely.

3 Sit up straight at table.

4 Wait to be served.

5 Finish all that is on your plate.

6 Use cutlery correctly.

7 Ask before you leave the table.

8 Don't interrupt unless it is very urgent.

9 Always say please and thank you.

10 Write to thank your host when you get home.